The Dandelion Seed's Big Dream

By Joseph Anthony
Illustrated by
Cris Arbo

DAWN PUBLICATIONS

To our children's children. — JA

To the people of Charlottesville, Virginia,
my favorite city. — CA

Library of Congress Cataloging-in-Publication Data

Anthony, Joseph (Joseph Patrick)
  The dandelion seed's big dream / by Joseph Anthony ; illustrations by Cris Arbo. -- First edition.
      pages cm
  Summary: A seed dreams of becoming a dandelion.
  ISBN 978-1-58469-496-0 (hardback) -- ISBN 978-1-58469-497-7 (pbk.) [1. Seeds--Fiction. 2. Dandelions--Fiction.] I. Arbo, Cris, illustrator. II. Title.
  PZ7.A6285Dc 2014
  [E]--dc23
                            2013050074

Book design and computer production by Patty Arnold, *Menagerie Design and Publishing*
Illustration photographs by Bill Moretz, *ProCamera*, Charlottesville, Virginia

Manufactured by Regent Publishing Services, Hong Kong,
Printed July, 2014, in ShenZhen, Guangdong, China
10 9 8 7 6 5 4 3 2 1
First Edition

DAWN PUBLICATIONS

12402 Bitney Springs Road
Nevada City, CA 95959
530-274-7775
nature@dawnpub.com

Once a little seed
took to the sky.

It had a dream.

Golden rays
from the sun
touched it.

Anything seemed possible as it soared above the earth.

But the wind shifted.

The seed got caught
in a very sticky place.
The rain, the sun, and
the rich, soft earth
seemed far away.

Still it held onto its dream of becoming a flower, like its parents, and their parents before.

Then the little seed
got badly hurt.
It almost lost its parachute.

I had no way of knowing
what was ahead.

Shadows fell.

It drifted through
a dark cave,

and out the other side
over the rooftops.

Its journey through the sky was almost over.

The seed landed in a very strange spot. Its worn out parachute tumbled away. Now what was to become of the broken little seed?

It waited, all alone, for a
long, long time.

It seemed to wait forever. But the
seed would not let go of its dream.

Then one day
it dropped to
the ground.

Suddenly it got an extra push. Home at last!
It knew just what to do.

Right then and there, the little seed started to grow.

Community Gardens

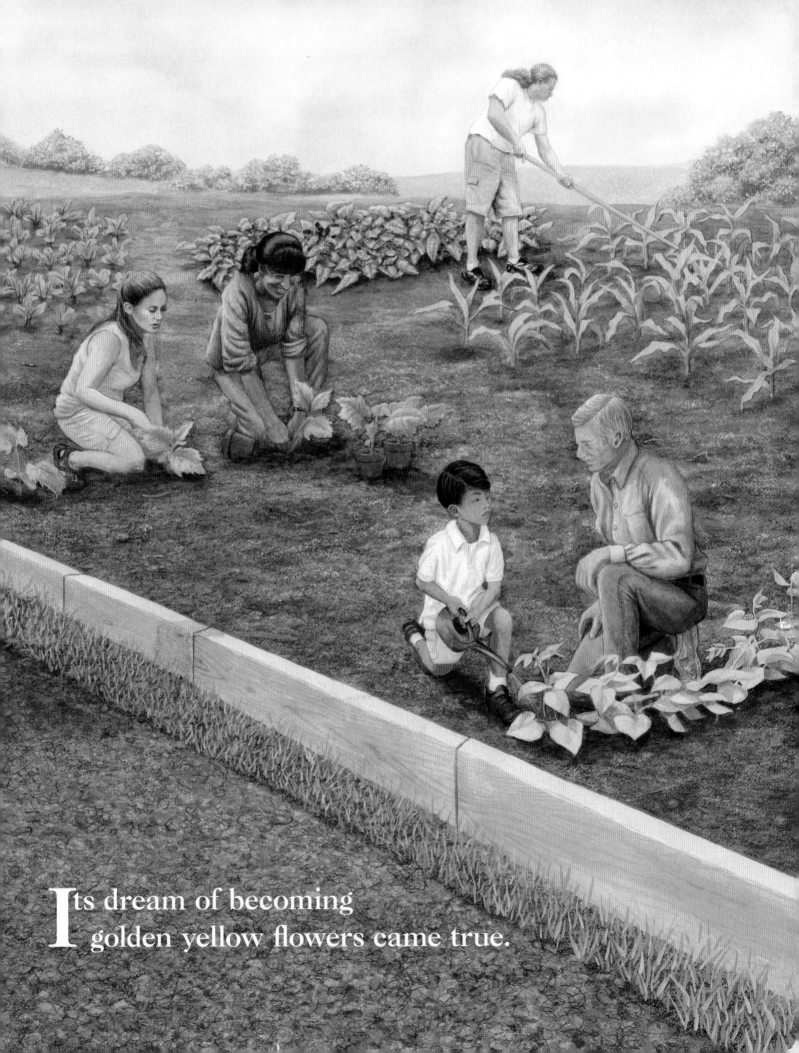

Its dream of becoming
golden yellow flowers came true.

Soon many more seeds filled the sky again. Each one had a dream.

They bloomed in their own time.

And each one made the world more beautiful.

Just Dandy!

🔹 DANDELIONS can be found in temperate climates in every continent except Antarctica. They thrive in sunny lawns and pastures, but they also grow in conditions where other plants can't survive, such as cracks in a sidewalk.

These hardy plants are *perennials*—they sprout up year after year from the same single long root (similar to a carrot). Their green leaves act like a funnel, catching raindrops and directing water to the plant's roots. The edges of the leaves are jagged, or toothed, giving the dandelion its name from the French *dents de lion*, "teeth of the lion." One or more hollow stems grow from the center of the leaves topped by a yellow flower. Actually, it's not just one flower but many little flowers called *florets* which together form a *composite flower* head.

After all of the florets bloom, the dandelion closes up and each floret forms a seed attached to a tuft of fine hairs on a stalk, like a parasail. When all of the seeds are mature, the dandelion opens up to reveal many fluffy, white seeds just waiting for the wind to blow. Individual seeds may travel as far as five miles away from the plant! A good way to appreciate this process is to watch a time-lapse video. Several wonderful videos are available on www.youtube.com. Search for "dandelion flower time lapse."

FLOWERS—composite head with many small florets

SEED HEADS—mature seeds attached to a fluffy tuft

SEEDS—travel on the wind

STEMS—contain a milky substance

LEAVES—toothed edges give the dandelion its name

ROOT—a long "taproot" supports the plant and draws in water and nutrients

Flower or Weed?

Some people see the dandelion as a flower whose yellow petals brighten yards, meadows, and roadsides. Others see it as a weed and try to get rid of it. As Ralph Waldo Emerson said, "Weediness is in the eye of the beholder."

Flower is a botanical term that refers to the part of the plant that produces seeds.

Weed is a term used to identify an unwanted or undesirable plant.

Dandelions were first brought to North America from Europe in the 1700s as food or medicine. Even today, dandelion leaves are eaten raw or cooked, and the roots boiled as a vegetable or roasted and ground to make a coffee substitute. A yellow dye can be made from the dandelion flower, and the white milky substance in the stem can be used to make a kind of glue. And it's not just people who use dandelions. Ninety-three species of insects rely on the dandelion for food, including honeybees that gather dandelion nectar and pollen.

Nevertheless, some people think that dandelions are "ruining a nice green lawn." And gardeners have to deal with dandelions competing with other plants. Dandelions grow vigorously, and when pulled up, if part of the root remains in the ground it will continue growing. ***What do you think? Flower or weed?***

Theme

Courage, patience, and perseverance are some of the themes in *The Dandelion Seed's Big Dream*. The prequel to this book, *The Dandelion Seed* (Dawn Publications, 1997), suggests themes of wonder, beauty, courage, and acceptance. Use the dandelion seed's life cycle as portrayed in both books as a springboard for a discussion about these themes in your students' lives. To reinforce the message, make connections with books that have similar themes, such as *The Little Yellow Leaf* by Carin Berger (Greenwillow Books, 2008) and *Cloudette* by Tom Lichtenheld (Henry Holt, 2011).

DIY with Dandelions

Take a Closer Look— Find a lawn or field with dandelions and examine them with a hand lens. Try to count the florets and notice bees or other insects using the dandelion for food.

Far and Wide Seed Dispersal—Dandelion seeds are carried by the wind, floating on their tiny parasails. Collect a variety of plant seeds and have children examine them to discover how each seed moves. For example, maple tree seeds are blown by the wind like dandelion seeds, but they are more like helicopters than parasails. Seeds like cockleburs stick to animal fur and get carried to a new place. When animals eat berries, seeds are deposited in their droppings. A coconut, the seed of a palm tree, moves by floating on water. For detailed K-2 lessons about how seeds are dispersed, go to "inquiry-based unit plan library" on the CASES website, http://cases.soe. umich.edu/, and click on "Where Did the Trees in Our Playground Come From."

Dandelion Watch—A dandelion's entire life cycle can be as short as nine weeks under good weather conditions, and the bloom matures to seeds in as little as a week. This makes the dandelion a perfect plant for children to observe when learning about the life cycle of a plant. Have children visit the same plant every couple of days for three to four weeks. They can record their observations in a science journal through words, pictures, or photos. You may want to explain to students that scientists keep detailed records of when plants sprout, leaf out, flower, and set seeds. The study of plant life cycles is called *phenology*. Plant records give scientists clues about the health of an ecosystem and provide valuable data about the effects of climate change.

Dandelion Memories—Dandelions are so common, they often play a role in our hearts and memories. Have students interview a parent or grandparent about a special dandelion memory. As a follow-up, have children draw a picture of the experience to share with the person they interviewed.

PHOTO BY SUE MILES

JOSEPH PATRICK ANTHONY and **CRIS ARBO** are a husband and wife team. Besides creating a family together, they continue to produce books for children young and old.

Joseph was born the tenth of eleven children. His family loved the mountains, so exploring with his brothers and sisters nurtured an innate love for adventure and an appreciation for the natural world. He traveled with the Navy as a trumpet player, worked in a natural food store, as a Corrections Officer, a massage therapist, and a construction supervisor, experiences which have all served to deepen his self-understanding and perspective on the human condition. Joseph's cosmological work, "Our Multi-Tiered Universe," grew out of a desire to help move the planet to a clean energy future. His website is www.JosephPatrickAnthony.com.

Cris Arbo's art is known for intense detail and is created by hand with paints and pencils, without the use of a computer. It has appeared in books, magazines, calendars, cards, murals, animated feature films, TV shows, and commercials. Also a gifted vocalist, she has performed with the London Symphony and London Philharmonic Choirs. She has illustrated seven nature awareness children's books for Dawn Publications and is also a frequent presenter at schools and conferences. Cris' website is www.author-illustr-source.com/crisarbo.htm.

Other Books from the Cris & Joe Team

The Dandelion Seed—The dandelion seed clings to its home, but is blown away to see the world—which is bigger, more frightening, and more beautiful than it ever imagined. Its growth, life adventures, and its own seed offers a thoughtful metaphor of life. (Written by Joe, illustrated by Cris.)

In A Nutshell—This is a tale about life from a "tree's-eye" view. As a youngster the acorn faces its own challenges, but as a great oak it oversees a parade of people and activities below. Here, in luminous illustrations, is the life cycle of an oak—and how it supports life even after it is gone. (Written by Joe, illustrated by Cris.)

What's In the Garden?—Good food doesn't begin on a store shelf in a box. Healthy fruits and vegetables become much more interesting when children know where they come from. So what's in the garden? (Illustrated by Cris.)

All Around Me, I See—With eyes wide open to the wonders of nature, a child on a hike discovers that "a leaf is a boat for a beetle "and that "a nest is a cradle for eggs." Tired from her long walk, she sleeps—and in her dream she flies like a bird and marvels at the beauty around her. (Illustrated by Cris.)

In the Trees, Honey Bees—Inside-the-hive views of a wild colony of honey bees offer close-ups of the queen, the cells, even bee eggs. The detailed art shimmers with life, highlighting each hair or grain of pollen on the bees. A wild hive in a tree in her own backyard served as a model! (Illustrated by Cris.)

Earth Heroes: Champions of the Ocean—Jacques Cousteau, Eugene Clark (the Shark Lady) and six other eminent marine conservationists made a lasting contribution to the world. Their biographies in this illustrated chapter book are inspiring for students and adults alike. (Illustrated by Cris.)

DAWN PUBLICATIONS is dedicated to inspiring in children a deeper understanding and appreciation for all life on Earth. You can browse through our titles, download resources for teachers, and order at www.dawnpub.com or call 800-545-7475.